In loving memory of

Allison Leah Lewis

January 25, 1977– March 22, 2002

Hat Trick

n. Sports :

Three goals scored by one player,

as in ice hockey

Santa on skates

With an old hockey stick

The oldest saint

To score a hat trick

But that's not so hard

Or so I've been told

When you have an elf

Guarding the goal

My pink and purple panda

My green and yellow frog

An orange alligator

A polka dotted dog

My blue plaid hippopotamus

My big red rabbit, too

They all keep me company

Here in my rainbow zoo

I'm burping up burrito

Shoulda had a plain taquito

Refried beans and Spanish rice

Lotsa tea with lotsa ice

A sopapilla and tortilla

Hi my friend it's good to see ya
Would you join me here for dinner ?

It would be so very nice

We could share an enchilada

Or maybe an empanada

Guacamole or frijoles

Oh, our dinner won't be light

I know today is chili

And I know this poem's silly

But it will be so hot tamale

That today would be just right

AC/DC

I know you wont see me

Lighting up your lights

And turning on your TV

I am an electron

When you turn the switch on

I'll go just where you want

Unless a burned-out fuse says "

DON'T "

Has anyone seen my lovey ?

I'm ready to go to sleep

I need it so that I can pray

The Lord my soul to keep

I need it 'cause I'm ready

To rest my little head

Thank goodness mommy found it !

It was underneath the bed

A frog jumped over a stop sign

To see how high he could hop

But after he hopped

A traffic cop

Said you didn't come

To a complete stop

So he wrote him out a ticket

And he hopped on down the road

To the froggy traffic court

Or so I have been toad

Elevator, escalator

Walking up the stairs

It doesn't matter how I go

As long as I get there

Fast plane, slow train

Will take me anywhere

It doesn't matter how I go

As long as I get there

A horsey or a camel

Walking softly on the sand

Will take me where I want to go

Across this great big land

A boat upon the ocean or

A ship upon the sea

Wherever in the world you are

Is where I want to be

My mommy made me breakfast

Of biscuits, eggs, and ham

(No, they're not green eggs and ham,
thank you Sam I Am)

She took a piece of ham out

And trimmed off all the fat

It looked just like a seahorse

What do you think of that ?

Although it made my breakfast

Look really kind of neat

Seahorse ham for breakfast

I don't think that I can eat

Red bugs, bed bugs

Bugs that want to bite

Bugs that creep

And bugs that crawl

Or fly around the light

Some bugs you can see

And some are out of sight

Some come out at daylight

And some come out at night

Some bugs make you itch

And some bugs make you scratch

But I never saw a baby bug

Until I saw one hatch

Vermiculite, vermiculite

We're going to plant our seeds tonight

Seeds of blue and green and red

We'll plant them in our flower bed

We'll water, mulch, and

Shoo the birds

Then flowers will greet us

Without words

Chicken little, little chicken

Don't want you to be no

" Finger Lickin' "

I like chickens That cluck and squawk
(better watch out for the chicken
hawk !)

You lay eggs and I'll bake bread
Together we'll see

That we both get fed

Sunkist orange, Nehi grape,

RC cola too

You can drink them with a Moon Pie

A pickled egg will do

These are two of our favorite foods

Down here in the South

It don't matter how you eat them

You just stuff 'em in your mouth

Raw fish wrapped in seaweed

Dead squid rolled in rice

I don't thing that I can eat it

It doesn't smell so nice

I'm staring at my plate now

My food looks kind of mooshy

Back home they call it bait

Here they call it sushi

I'm going to talk to Norman

To see what he will say

Is it going to rain or snow

Tomorrow and today

If it snows I'll wear warm clothes

And go outside to play

But if it rains I'll stay inside

And watch cartoons all day

I went to see the doctor

Because my stomach hurt

I threw up in the bathroom

And got barf upon my shirt

Mom said I had a fever

That I was burning hot

She took me to the office

So I could get a shot

My doctor came into the room

And checked my ears and nose

She checked every part of me

From my head down to my toes

She checked my chest and

Checked my heart and

Checked my stomach, too

And when she looked into my throat

I thought that she was through

But then she checked my winkie

Which made me kind of blush

But nothing could compare to

When she checked my tush

So if you have a stomach ache

And throw up on your shirt

Don't ever tell your mommy

' Cause boy those shots do hurt !

Tick tock goes the clock

The one that's in the hall

It's an old grandfather clock

It makes me feel so small

I've been watching it for hours

Hoping I can see

The little mouse run up it

That's what daddy read to me

A nutty buddy for my buddy

A popsicle for me

Ice cream for my other friends

When they come home with me

Cookies, candy, cakes, and cokes

And sweet pickles, too

That is what we all will have

When we go home with you

A gnat flew by

It flew in my eye

It started to itch

I started to cry

My mom got a swatter

And hit the gnat with it

My eye hurt so bad

That she had to kith it

I lost a sock

I know not where

Now I have one

But not a pair

Where could it be ?

I think I know

Why should I debate it ?

I know just where to look for it

Of course, the dryer ate it !

A nascent car in NASCAR

Won't go too far

Not far enough to win a race

Or even come in second place

I've got a tickle in my throat

I'm afraid that I might choke

Then I cough and cough and cough

It made my tickle switch turn off

Then I sneeze and sneeze and sneeze

May I have a tissue, please ?

Little ducky, little ducky

Quack, quack, quack

Swimming in the pond

With a June bug on its back

" We must go home for dinner

When our swim is through

And if there's no one at my house

Then I'll go home with you "

Pink shoes, blue shoes

Little goody two shoes

Old shoes, new shoes

Little bitty feet shoes

Eight shoes, no shoes

Four shoes or two

A spider, snake, and zebra

Or a boy like me and you

There was a poor whale

Who got caught in the hail

It bounced of her head, her back,

And her tail

I know that this doesn't make

Very much sense

But now the poor whale

Is all covered with dents

Bryson is a frog expert

He knows them through and through

The ones in creeks and lakes and

Swamps in ponds and rivers, too

He knows how high they hop

He knows how far they jump

He knows how to catch them

While they're sitting on a stump

So if you have a question

' Bout that frog down by the creek

Chances are that Bryson

Has the answers that you seek

My daddy had a date

With Joyce Kilmer's sister

Before he met my mommy

He said he even kissed her

This is what he said to her

At least it's what he told me

" You're as lovely as a poem

But not as lovely as a tree "

Mommy drives a big black car

She drives it near

She drives it far

She drives it here

She drives it there

She drives her big car everywhere

She drives to town

She drives to school

She drives it to the swimming pool

When mommy drives her

Big black car

She feels just like a movie star

Sissy had an itchy fit

She squirmed a lot

She scratched a bit

She scratched her ears

She scratched her nose

She scratched her knees

She scratched her toes

She scratched her teeth

She scratched her hair

She scratched beneath

Her underwear !

Up the stairs and down the stairs

At daddy's beck and call

All because he wants to hang

Some pictures on the wall

'' Bring the hammer

Bring the nails

And bring the hangers, too ''

I'm going to need a big long nap

When this job is through !

Burgers, chicken, dogs, and chips

Cheese and ranch and onion dips

Baked beans, cole slaw, pickles, too

We'll bring them just to name a few

Horseshoes, bats, a ball and glove

And of course we'll bring

All the People we love

Litterbug, jitterbug

Dancing through the trash

If you throw it out the window

It'll cost you lots of cash

When you're finished

With your Burger

And your fries and cola, too

Just throw it in the trash can

I will be so proud of you !

Lobster man, lobster man

Looks like he was fried

In a frying pan

He only burns

He doesn't tan

Better stay in the shade

Lobster man

We went to see my mamaw

And to see my papaw, too

We went out for pizza

It's my favorite thing to do

I colored with my crayons

And I played with all my dolls

But my brother got in trouble

When he colored on the walls

I love to see my mamaw

And to see my papaw, too

And they both go straight to bed

When our visit's through

Ethan and Sam

Went out to play

In their back yard

One sunshiny day

Sam said to Ethan

" It's your turn to hide "

But he couldn't find him

Poor Sam, he just cried

Leo likes his cookies

He has a favorite kind

To know just what it is

You don't have to read his mind

If he asks you for a cookie

You'd better get it right

Give Leo an Oreo

Or he might cry all night

The Children's Poem

What's in a name ?

This poem will tell

All one must know is

The name how to spell

Our children's names

Are found just below

And their names' meanings

Soon you will know

Regina's our queen

And Stephen's her king

Allison and Margaret

Their precious pearl do bring

Daniel has judged

That Mark's warlike spectre

Must yield to William

Their kingdom's protector

The Cleaning Lady's poem

(with apologies to Toody and

Muldoon)

The bedroom's a disaster

And the kitchen looks a fright

And if my mom comes over

She will say " My, what a sight "

Why the living room's a mess

Well, it's anybody's guess

Amber, where are you ?

Maggie's Poem

Chicken booty dee dee

I think you will see me

Looking for the paint brush

The one that makes my cheeks blush

Papa Rick and Alice

Brought my family to the palace

Down here by the sea, see ?

Chicken booty dee dee

Allison's Poem

You were my dear baby

I was just a baby, too

We grew up together

It was always me and you

Like Vincent in the song

I know that this is true

This world was never meant for one

As beautiful as you

Made in the USA
Middletown, DE
02 September 2021